Stories That Should Be Told

Timeless Parables For Modern Souls

Kenneth Willers

FREILING
AGENCY

First Paperback and Hardback Editions

Some names, businesses, places, events, locales, incidents, and identifying details inside this book have been changed to protect the privacy of individuals.

Published by Freiling Agency, LLC.

P.O. Box 1264
Warrenton, VA 20188

www.FreilingAgency.com

PB ISBN: 978-1-963701-13-5
HB ISBN: 978-1-963701-12-8
E-book ISBN: 978-1-963701-11-1

In the Beginning

Introduction

Move On

Student:	"You've done so many things in your life—when did you know it was right to move on to a new road?"
Master:	"I've never moved on to a new road."
Student:	"But you've done so many different things, gone to so many different places. Surely, you must have changed roads when you knew it was time to move on."
Master:	"Never! I have never changed my road, I have always let my road change me, and then I moved on."

I wrote "Move On" in the spring of 1990 when I made a decision that would change the course of my life forever, and end up deeply influencing my understanding of leadership and the power of storytelling.

Many of the short, parable-like stories you will encounter in this collection were written over thirty years ago at a pivotal time in my life. I was a student at the Jesuit School of Theology with the Graduate Theological Union in Berkeley, CA, discerning, after eight years of seminary studies, if I would proceed to the priesthood. As part of my Master of Divinity requirements, I enrolled in a scripture class focused on the Gospel parables and taught by Fr. John Donahue, S.J. For our mid-term exam, Fr. John assigned a twenty-five-page paper analyzing a single parable of our choosing. After the collective groan of the class, he posed an intriguing challenge: "If anyone would like to write and submit a parable in lieu of the term paper, I will offer you that challenge." He assured us it might be easier to write the paper.

I accepted the challenge. In fact, after I completed one parable, I continued to write two additional ones and then created a "narrative" in which I embedded the three parables, fashioning my transcription after how the Gospel narratives were constructed. At the end of the term, Fr. John handed me back my submission along with a two-page single-typed letter in which he graciously complimented my parables, reflected on their meaning, and encouraged me to continue writing. The parables I turned in that day served as the catalyst to *Move On*, knowing that I had been transformed by the road and that my future would now take me in a new direction. Furthermore, because of that class and the encouragement from Fr. John, I authored over 100 stories. I am delighted to share forty of them with you in this collection.

Stories have long held a revered place in human history, serving as a powerful tool for communication and connection. In the realm of leadership, storytelling plays a crucial role in shaping the experiences of all stakeholders. The impact of storytelling is profound, as it can spark curiosity, evoke emotions, and foster a deeper understanding of complex concepts. Stories can also speak in ways that provide comfort, meaning, and purpose when the events of life render the most heartfelt words void of impact.

I recall September 11, 2001. I was just nine days into my new role as a first-time principal at St. John's Elementary Catholic School in the Glen Park area of San Francisco. I always arrived early and on this particular morning, I was listening to news on talk radio and was stunned by what was being reported. Soon after the first plane hit at 8:46 AM EST (5:46 AM in California) I walked into one of the classrooms to turn on the TV. I remember standing there in shock while I watched in real time the second plane barrel into the adjacent tower. Not long after, local news reports were suggesting that a plane was headed toward SF. By 6:30 AM PST, the mayor of SF ordered all the schools in SF to be closed. Fortunately, the only students on campus were our early daycare children, numbering about thirty-five. For parents who were not aware of the mayor's mandate, I instructed my staff to greet families at our drop-off points and inform them that the school was closed. By 10 AM, all the students were safely with the parents.

Now the emotions of that day, the fear, the sadness, and the anger, were setting in and I knew

I had to reach out to my parent community with words of comfort and hope. I could not find the words. So, for the first time in over fifteen years, I turned to one of my stories for insight. The next day, I shared with the families the following story I had written over a decade earlier, along with my best attempt at a concluding reflection:

The Glass Is Already Broken

Once Upon a Time,

...a man went to get himself a glass of water and as he picked up the glass, the glass said, "Stop, look at me. Don't you see I am already broken?"

"What?" the man said, "You are in perfect condition."

"Regardless," answered back the glass, "I will be of no use to you—I am already broken."

"Nonsense," the man thought and he filled up the glass with water and said, "See, you hold the water wonderfully -- not one drop leaks out."

"Take a better look," said the glass, "and you will see I am already broken."

Holding the glass to the light the man said, "Ridiculous, see how the light shines through your glass and water—it sparkles and shines. You're beautiful and your glass possesses no cracks."

"But, don't you see, sir," repeated the glass, "I am already broken."

"No, you're not," barked the man and he drank the water from the glass.

"See? Perfect. You are perfect." And he placed the glass carefully back on the shelf. Before he left the room, he took one more look at the glass and asked it, "Why do you keep saying you're broken when you're not?"

"How else will you see me?" responded the glass.

"Excuse me?" said the man, "I don't understand."

"How many times have you picked me up and drank from me?" asked the glass.

"Hundreds of times," answered the man.

"Exactly!" was the glass's sharp reply. "And you never once saw my beauty. But this time, because you were afraid I was broken, you took time to look at me and you saw how precious I really am. If that's what it takes to get your attention, then remember, this glass is already broken."

In light of the pain our nation and our community have experienced these past few days, let us hold our children close to our hearts and give thanks to God for our most precious gifts of life. Because our gift is so fragile we must always hold and see the ones we love first and foremost in our minds and hearts. Our daily "routine" seems small and insignificant when compared with the potential loss of those we love. Together, let us reassure our children that they are safe and well cared for.

Let us pray that our world leaders inspire hope and calm to a nation in grief and let us remember the victims, their families and the tremendous loss of life in our prayers and thoughts. Finally, let us give thanks for those who, right now, are risking their lives to restore safety to our fragile global village.

Although the "glass is already broken," let us try to see our brothers and sisters in pain as vessels of our collective and unbreakable human spirit reminding the world that, as we stand in solidarity, we do so with our deep trust in the merciful providence of God.

I discovered, the following day, that by using this story to reach out to my parent community, I offered them more than just the opportunity to reflect on the events that occurred. I gifted them with a metaphor that reminded all of us, including myself, about those we hold precious in our lives.

The story, while intended to provide comfort to my parents, offered me a deeper insight into the transformative power of story.

Let me conclude my introduction with this, by engaging the "listeners" in narratives that resonate with their interests and experiences, storytellers can create an immersive environment that provokes cathartic emotions, inspires curiosity, fuels engagement, and will even challenge the status quo. Through the art of storytelling, leaders can cultivate a sense of community in the workplace, the conference room, the boardroom, and the classroom, or wherever the "listeners" feel valued, understood, and empowered to explore new ideas and perspectives.

In sharing these stories, my hope is that you find inspiration and wisdom that resonate deeply with your own journey. Let the narratives serve as a guide, illuminating the path toward growth, transformation, and the profound realization that we never truly move on to a new road; instead, we let our road change us, and then we move onward, enriched by the experiences that shape our journey.

Once A Lazarus, Like Me

Your brother couldn't see me because he forgot what Moses and the Prophets had said, and yet, I was there at the gate everyday trying to help him remember. One day I was so weak that I even laid down in front of the gate so he'd have to step over me and surely see me. But he sent out his dogs to chase me away. Well, at least they stopped to lick my sores—he, well, he just passed me by. Lazarus had forgotten who I was.

I understand he was a busy man and very important to the community. He was well liked—or so it seemed because he had many friends. Once, I peeked into his house during a celebration where there were many of his friends—the food he served was unbelievable. I thought if I could only hide under the table then I could eat the pieces of bread the guests were throwing aside, the dogs were even lucky enough to feast upon that.

Yet I couldn't blame him. He had worked hard to build up his walls of wealth. You would have thought that God most certainly had blessed him. And me, well, sometimes people would pass me at the gate and say, "You lazy wretch, why don't you hire yourself out for work, instead of lying here all day." What really hurt me about your brother was that he never saw me. He never once spoke to me or even really looked at me.

It was as if there were a huge wall or great chasm that separated our worlds that made any interchange between the two of us impossible. Yet there we were occupying the same space, but perhaps for him the way we were occupying it was the cause for distance. I really don't know.

The last thing I remember was falling asleep very hungry and cold, like I had for many nights, but when I awoke this time I was surrounded by the warmth of our Father Abraham's embrace. You know this was the first time I experienced being touched. And the sores on my body seemed to heal.

Then, my memory about how life was on earth while I was alive seemed to disappear—it's funny isn't it, how, when all is well, we forget our painful past. And I realize now that it must be very hard to be compassionate to others in pain when we forget our own. Anyway, when I heard the voice of your brother I was startled by it—I looked up and there he was way across a great abyss, no longer clothed in purple, no, now he was wrapped in flames and he was calling out to Abraham for help.

At first, I thought it strange that although I was in full view of him—he never spoke directly to me—he was asking Abraham for my help. It became obvious to me that he still didn't want to see me. He wanted me to go to you and to his other brothers and sisters and warn them—yet, he never asked me. "Don't I have a voice?" I thought. "Am I still invisible to you even in death? Don't you remember who I am yet?" So, Abraham took care of it. I just listened and felt pity.

However, since then, enough time has passed. I just couldn't be silent any longer. I had to come back and speak to his brothers and sisters before it was too late.

Listen! I can only say this once—remember! Your memory will be your salvation! Remember your ancestors who lived as slaves and peasants in a foreign land; who walked as homeless people for many years in search of comfort; who immigrated to a new land for freedom and a new life. Do you remember how often they relied on the kindness of strangers and on the generosity of God's love through the goodness of others to survive?

Remember because now you have a responsibility to live out of that memory. Brothers and sisters of the rich man, please understand that the wealthy walls we sometimes build can silence our crying memory or blind us from what we once were. And this causes us not to see the face or hear the voice of the poor person that is at our own gate. Remember! And then I'll be seen—then, I'll be heard.

It's really very simple to look around your house, or office; look around your families and communities. Go out to the city streets, or to the fields, visit the prisons, or the immigration offices—tear down your rich arrogant walls that separate and silence others and build humble bridges across the abyss—because then you'll see me—because then and only then will I have a voice worth hearing, and I won't be invisible anymore. First, however, you must remember. You must remember that you, too, were once a Lazarus like me.

I Am An Ant

Once Upon a Time, there was an apprentice ant who was interrupted from his studies by an older ant who asked him, “On the basis of what you’ve been taught, who are you?”

The apprentice ant thought for a moment and said, “I have learned that, in comparison to the rest of the world, I am very small.”

“Very good!” The older ant replied, and before leaving he told the apprentice ant to continue his studies.

A year passed and the apprentice ant grew in size and knowledge. It came to pass that the same old ant came to him again, interrupted his studies, and asked him, “On the basis of what you’ve been taught, who are you?”

The apprentice ant thought for a moment and said, “I have learned that not only am I very small in comparison to the rest of the world, but I am also able to carry many times my own weight.”

"Very good!" The older ant replied, and before leaving he told the apprentice ant to continue his studies.

Now, many years had past and the apprentice ant had grown even more in size and knowledge. On the day the apprentice ant finished his training, the old ant came to him again, interrupted his studies, and asked him, "On the basis of what you've been taught, who are you?"

The ant thought for a moment and said, "I have learned that not only am I very small in comparison to the rest of the world, or able to carry many times my own weight, I know that **I am an Ant**!"

The old ant was horrified by this for he had never heard this teaching before. The old ant asked the once apprentice ant where he learned this. The young ant responded,

"I have come to this knowledge on my own."

Outraged by this ant's arrogance the older ant had him killed for he was afraid this new knowledge would spread throughout the colony.

Vocations

Once Upon A Time, there was a monastery where the brothers who lived there worked on a little field and they were neither happy nor sad. They were, you could say, indifferent. The brothers had all settled down to this way of life and work for they didn't know any other way of living.

One day a very smart and talented young man came to the monastery and wanted to join the brothers. The young man had great abilities in writing, music, the arts, and the sciences. The Abbot felt very lucky that such a young man wanted to join the brothers.

As his training was coming to an end, the young man went to his Abbot and asked, "Should I continue my studies as a writer?"

"Oh no," said the Abbot, "one does not write here. All we do here is care for our little field."

"I see." said the young man, and he went out into the field.

More time went by and the young man returned to the Abbot and asked, "Should I continue my studies in music and the arts?"

"Oh no," said the Abbot, "that would be of no use here for all we do is care for our little field."

"I see." said the young man, and he went back out into the field.

A year went by and the young man returned to the Abbot again. "Should I continue my studies in science and technology?"

"Oh no," said the Abbot, "don't you understand that all we do here is work in our little field and you must settle for that and nothing more."

"I see." said the young man, and he went back out into the field.

As the young man was working in the field, he found an old box buried deep in the earth. He opened the box and inside was a picture of a monastery where the brothers were smiling, singing, playing, working, building, studying, and praying. In the front of all the activity was a young man who was obviously the Abbot. The young man thought to himself, "*This is the monastery I want to join.*"

So, the young man went to the Abbot with the picture and said, "Father, I must leave here at once for I have found the monastery God has called me to join."

The Abbot asked, "What monastery is this?"

The young man gave the Abbot the picture and said, "Here it is. I found it in the little field as I was digging. You can have it. Now, I must move on. Good-bye."

The Abbot cried as he looked at the picture for he remembered his founder with love.

His Reflection

Once Upon A Time, in an old native village there lived a group of women who would listen attentively as the wise sage taught the men of the village about a mystical river that gave forth the Water of Eternal Life and Happiness. These women marveled at his words and would often talk about the mystical river among themselves. After the wise sage stopped speaking and the men went back to their huts to pray, the women stayed behind and, out of love, would cook for the wise sage, mend his clothes, soothe his aches, and sit in silence with him when he prayed.

One day, to the surprise of all the villagers, the wise sage was nowhere to be found. The women were very troubled by his absence and the men of the village began to doubt that they would ever find the mystical river he spoke about. So, filled with despair, the men went back to their huts to pray. The women, however, went out into the forest to search for the wise sage pretending that they were going to collect wood for their stoves.

As they walked through the forest they would call out his name, but there was no response. Stopping to rest and quiet themselves for a while before they returned to the village, they heard the sound of water flowing. The sound was very faint and gentle.

They listened to the sound and followed its direction and it led them to the banks of a beautiful river that extended for miles in every direction. As they peered into the water, however, they did not see their own reflection but they saw the reflection of the sage. They knew, now, that this was the mystical river he so often spoke about.

Excited by their discovery they ran back to the village with the good news of their discovery. The men of the village at first did not believe the women but they agreed to follow them to the river. When they saw the river for themselves, saw how beautiful it was, and peered into it to see the reflection of the sage, they believed.

Not long after the men took over the banks of the river and would not allow the women access the river. The men of the village justified this rule by saying, “It was in our reflection the wise sage appeared when we looked into the water, and besides the wise sage only taught us men about this mystery and not you women.” So, from that time on, if the women wanted water they would first have to go to the men of the village and ask if they might receive this gift from the river.

I Wonder

For the Fool: "I wonder" usually means: I can't accept what my mind is not able to wrap around and smother.

For the Wise: "I wonder" means: I'm in awe of what is able to wrap itself around my mind and yet not smother it.

In the first case wonder produces suspicion.
In the second case wonder produces enlightenment.

The Well That Never Runs Dry

Once Upon A Time, there was a good and generous king who possessed a mystical well. The king loved and cared for the well very much because the well promised that it would never run dry as long as its water was used for the good of the kingdom. Because of this promise, the king and all the people in the kingdom were very happy.

Many years passed and the king needed to go to other countries and search for new mystical wells. The king, upon the eve of his departure, called for his servants and put them in charge of the well during his absence. He told them that the water in the well would never run dry as long as they used the water for the good of the kingdom. The servants then promised to care for the well and the kingdom while the king was away, and the king set off on his journey.

The abundance of water from the well was overwhelming to the servants. No matter how much water they gave to the people the well never seemed to run dry. Many years passed and the servants began to take this tremendous water source for granted. The servants began to think that since the king was away and the water was so plentiful, "Why don't we use this water as a means to build up some security for ourselves for the future. That way, when the king returns we will be able to take care of ourselves."

So, they began to waste the water on their own fields, they began to limit the water for the people in the kingdom, and finally, they began to sell the water to people in nearby villages for their own profit. Because of this abuse the water source in the well began to diminish. But the servants were so taken up with their new source of income and security that they lost sight of the water level.

One day, during the height of their wealth, they received a message from the king saying he would be returning in three day's time and was looking forward to seeing his well.

The servants then went and hid all their money, ran to the well and cleaned all around it so the king would not be angry to see how uncared for it was—but, when they looked into the well and saw how low the water level was, they thought for sure they would be killed upon the king's return.

The only way to solve the problem, they thought, was to buy water from the nearby villages and pour into the well until it was full again. After collecting all the money they had acquired during the king's absence, they bought as much water as their money would buy. But after pouring into the well, they saw that it was not enough. So, they then went into every house and stole water from every person in the village—but it still was not enough. Next, the servants even killed some people in order to get more water—but all these attempts were in vain for the water level would not rise.

In the midst of all this frenzy, the king returned. When he saw the people, and the empty well, he knew what had happened. He had his guards bring the servants before him and had them tortured. He then told the servants that they would never have access to the well again. Then, the king had the servants banished from the kingdom. The king was sad because he knew the well had been lost forever and the people of the kingdom would now suffer for the rest of their lives.

The king then sat by the dry well and, looking down into its depths, he cried. He cried and cried until his tears filled the well. Once the well was full, he appointed new servants and commanded them to take care of this well because he had to leave to make sure that his other wells were being better cared for.

The Closed Hand

Once Upon A Time there was a religious man who held a dime very tightly in his hand, and he thought he was poor. Then the man thought to become even poorer he'd drop his dime and his hand would be empty. Once his dime was gone and his hand was empty he closed his hand tightly around its emptiness. He was proud because he could hold on to his poverty so tightly.

And yet, the poorest man I ever saw was standing on a corner and his hand was open.

The Beautiful and Mystical River

Once Upon A Time, there was a man who went on a journey in search of a beautiful and mystical river. When he found the river, he sat down next to it, he drank from it, he bathed in it, he fished from it, he played in it, and he even nearly drowned in it. This man was filled with joy just by being with the river. The man stayed many days and nights with the river and listened to its mystical teachings. Before he left he painted a picture of the river and then set off for home.

Upon his return his family, friends, and the townspeople, all noticed the joy this man now possessed and asked him what had happened to him at the river. They asked him many questions about the river and wanted to know what mystical teachings he had learned.

The man told them, "You must go for yourselves and experience this river. You must see, listen, touch, taste, and smell the river for yourselves for

I could never fully describe or hope to explain the beauty or the mystery I experienced from this river. Words could never say it all…I urge you, go! Experience the river yourselves."

Instead, the people found the man's painting of the river and took it from him. They said, "The secret of the river is hidden within this painting." So they put the painting into a special golden frame, built a large building, and hung the painting on the wall so they could come and gaze at the picture, hoping to find its secret. The man, seeing what had happened, was sad and he wished he had never painted that picture of the beautiful and mystical river.

Books and Wells

Once Upon A Time, there was a man who said he wanted to search for deep wells. Before he set out to seek his desire, he thought it would first be wise to consult all the great books that had been written on the subject of deep wells. The man read many books on where to find wells and the differences in depth that they possessed. One day, while he was strolling casually along, engrossed in his reading of wells, he failed to notice a large deep well right in front of him. When he bumped into the deep well, his book flew from his hands and fell quite far into the deep recesses of the well. The man, quite upset at the loss, frantically lowered a nearby bucket to retrieve his book, but his attempt was in vain. The man went away very sad that he lost his book, for he thought, without his book, how could he ever be able to find a deep well.

The Gold Box

I once saw a man slap his brother with words of cruel judgment—then go into a church, bow before a gold box, and pray for forgiveness.

Again, I saw the same man starve his brother with the negligence of an apathetic mind—then go into a church, bow before a gold box, and pray for forgiveness.

Then, I saw this same man kill his brother with the coldness of a selfish heart—then go into a church, bow before a gold box, and pray for forgiveness.

I'm curious, what does this man see in the gold box that he doesn't see in his brother?

Agree to Disagree

Once Upon A Time, there were three tailors who were very dedicated to making clothes. They prided themselves on how well they got along with each other because they agreed never to disagree.

One day a man came in and asked if he could have a pair of pants made for him. The first tailor looked at the man and from sight attempted to guess his size. The second tailor also looked at the man and from sight attempted to guess his size. It didn't take long before the two tailors soon realized that they both had come to different sizes so, rather than have a disagreement, they agreed to divide the pants in half, each making one side. The third tailor, however, took a measuring tape and sized up the man. When he told the other two tailors that both were wrong with their sizes, he was immediately fired for he had broken their agreement not to disagree.

A few days later, the man returned to pick up his new pants and after he tried them on he found that one leg was too short and the other was too long. The pants were obviously of no use to him, and, angered by this mistake, he canceled his order, refused to pay for the pants, and never did business with them again.

A Piece of Glass

There once was a sharp piece of glass lying on the ground, shimmering in full view of all who passed it. Everybody who passed this sharp piece of glass just avoided it because they were afraid they would be cut if they picked it up.

It so happened that one day as a young woman was walking along she noticed on the ground a beautiful piece of glass shimmering and sparkling in the sunlight. The young woman marveled at the splendor of this piece of glass and bent down to pick it up.

As she picked up the piece of glass, she clutched it in her hand and the piece of glass cut her giving her a deep wound. The young woman dropped the piece of glass and started to cry. Her tears as well as her blood dripped onto the piece of glass and the piece of glass started to speak.

"Why didn't you just leave me alone on the ground if you didn't want to get cut?" Asked the piece of glass.

The young woman responded, "You are so beautiful in the light, I wanted to hold you. Tell me, why did you cut me?"

The piece of glass answered, "You held on too tightly. If you still want to experience me, pick me up gently, and hold me up to the light—then you will see how beautiful I really am."

The young woman did what the piece of glass had said. She marveled again at the sight and said, "You know, you are very beautiful, how can it be then, that your beauty has the power to wound?"

The piece of glass responded, "My beauty only wounds when people hold on to it too tightly and try to make it their own."

The Crutch and the Healer

There once was a man who broke his leg, so he went to a crutch maker and bought himself a crutch to lean on. Time passed and since the man didn't know his leg had healed he kept using the crutch for something to lean on.

One day a healer came to the village where the man lived and told the man to trust him, give up his crutch, and walk. The man threw down his crutch and walked.

Now the man leans on the Healer.

Ignorant and Foolish

There once was a teacher who spent all his time teaching the great mysteries of life to others who he considered ignorant and foolish.

One day, however, this teacher met up with the wisest man in the world. The wise man was sitting by the edge of a river contemplating nature, as wise men often do, but much to the surprise of the teacher, this wise man was also watching a young boy splash about in the water.

The teacher, wanting to share his knowledge with the wise man, said, "Come with me, sir, let us speak someplace where we won't be disturbed by this foolish and ignorant youth."

The wise man, however, ignored the teacher's comment. He just sat in silence and watched the boy play in the water until his mother called him away. After the boy was gone, the teacher asked the wise man why he wasted his time watching this ignorant and foolish boy play in the water when there was so much to learn.

"Oh, but I have learned something," said the wise man. "I learned something more profound than any book could ever hope to teach."

"What is that?" asked the teacher.

"I have learned," said the wise man, "that the greatest obstacle to wisdom is assuming that others are more ignorant and foolish than oneself. For the wise, everyone becomes a teacher."

Silence

S*omeone once* told me that God could only be heard in silence. If by silence, however, you mean shutting off others and muting out those around me, how should I ever hear God?

God's Voice

Once Upon A Time, a young monk wanting to hear God's voice speaking in his life asked his abbot if he could go on a silent retreat until God spoke to him. The abbot agreed and told the young monk, "Now, be attune to all around you—then, nothing will distract you and you'll hear God's voice for sure."

Now, God was also very pleased with the resolve of this young monk. So pleased, in fact, that God sent a messenger down to earth to speak to the young monk. When the messenger saw the young monk sitting all alone in the garden waiting to hear God's voice, he went up to the young monk and said, "You are very lucky, my friend, God wishes to speak with you."

"I know," said the young monk. "Now, will you please go away or be quiet. Can't you see I am trying to be attuned to all around me and how can I hear God's voice if you're talking to me. Now, be quiet!"

God's Voice

Once upon a time a young monk wanting to hear God's voice speaking in his life asked his abbot if he could go on a silent retreat until God spoke to him. The abbot agreed and told the young monk, "Now be attentive to all around you—then nothing will distract you and you'll hear God's voice for sure."

Now God was, so we're told, pleased with the resolve of this young monk. So pleased, in fact, that God sent a messenger down to convey a message to the young monk. When the messenger saw the young monk kneeling alone in the garden, waiting to hear God's voice, he went up to the young monk and said, "You are very lucky, my friend. God wishes to speak with you."

"I know," said the young monk. "Now, will you please go away or be quiet. Can't you see that I'm trying to be attentive to all around me? How can I hear God's voice if you're talking to me? Away with you! Be off!"

His House

Once Upon A Time, there was a poor boy who had nothing he could call his own. He always relied on the generosity of others to live and he hated this dependence. So, as he got older he worked very hard, saved his money and eventually became a very rich and self-sufficient man.

Not long after his financial success, he built himself a special house. Special because, when completed, his house would possess everything he would ever need and, that way he thought, he would never have to be dependent on anyone ever again. His house was splendid indeed, in fact, it was the largest in the village. People from all around marveled at its size and grandeur, and yet, they wondered how he would afford its maintenance.

Remembering his promise never to rely on others again, he cemented his doors shut so he could never leave, and he painted pictures over all the windows so no one could ever look in. He was very happy indeed because he thought now he was self-sufficient.

Because his house was so big it needed large amounts of electric power and fuel. As a result, all the smaller homes in the town began to lose the little power they had to fuel his house. Because his house needed so much water to fill its pools and baths and to care for its plants and fields all the other smaller homes began to lose the little water they had to his large reservoirs. And, because his house needed so much food to last a lifetime, all the smaller homes in the town had to eat even less because of his needs.

As the man sat in his house with its unlimited power, endless water, and ample food supply, he thought to himself, "How happy I am! Happy, because with my new house, I will never ever have to take anything from anyone ever again."

The Parable of the Two Sons

The priests and religious leaders came up to the prophet again and asked him why he wanted nothing to do with the institutions that his forefathers had built and took pride in creating, and they questioned him on why he insisted on teaching and ministering outside the already established circles. Upon seeing them, the prophet turned to them and told them this parable.

A Man had two sons. The first-born son was by far the man's favorite. The first son's birth had come easy, his face was handsome to behold for he took on the features of his father. The man spent much time with his first son for he was just like his father. The first son grew to be strong and self-sufficient. The neighbors marveled at the love this man showed toward his first son for the man was very proud of his first-born son. When it was time for the son to leave home the man was very sad.

Upon the first son's departure the man's second son was born. This birth was very rough. The son's face was troublesome to behold for his features were foreign and quite unlike his father's. The man neglected his second son for he was different, and began to busy himself with the life and family of the first son. The second son grew weak and insecure. At this, the neighbors all worried because of the man's neglect, and while the man was away they came and took the second son from the man's house to care for him and raise him as a real son. The man, on returning home, wasn't sad for he never noticed the second son's absence.

At this, the priests and religious leaders left and began to murmur about this prophet among themselves.

A Dead Mouse

A man once said to me, "We have a dead mouse in our house, it really smells and we can't find it."

I responded, "Why don't you get a cat to find the mouse?"

The man answered back, "We can't do that, we're allergic to cats."

I replied, "I see, then, I hope you get used to the smell."

Two Trees

Once Upon A Time, there were two trees. The first tree said to the second tree, "Why don't we plant ourselves over there by the river because there's plenty of water and lots of sun."

"Good idea," the second tree said. "But I want the spot closest to the river."

And the second tree raced in front of the first tree and planted itself closest to the river. So, the first tree had to stretch its roots very far to get enough water to grow.

Time passed and the first tree said, "Doesn't the sun feel wonderful on our branches?"

"Yes," said the second tree, "and since I am able to get more water, I'm going to grow faster and I'll get more of the sun."

And the second tree grew very fast and straight and blocked much of the sun from the first tree. So, the first tree had to bend and curve and weave itself around the other tree just to get a little sun on each of its branches.

Time passed and the first tree said, "I didn't realize how many birds want to use our branches for homes."

"I know," said the second tree. "That is why I have made my branches long and sparse so they won't build their homes on me."

And the second tree remained empty of any bird life, just as he hoped it would be. So, instead, all the birds in the area built their homes on the first tree because his branches were bushy, curved, and stout.

Time passed and the first tree said, "I think I see some lumberjacks heading in our direction, but it's hard to see from my position."

"Yes," said the second tree, "you're right, I can see them good because I am straight and tall, not short and curved, I am well-trimmed, not bushy, and I have no birds to block my view."

And the second tree was proud of his appearance. So, the first tree worried that he would be chapped down because he wasn't like the second tree.

When the lumberjacks arrived, they stopped in awe of the first tree for they had never seen a tree that was shaped so oddly, with curved limbs, bushy leaves, and with so much life in its branches.

They thought, "Such a beautiful and rare tree should not be chopped down."

Then, looking at the second tree that was tall, slim, straight, and not too bushy, they thought, "Such a straight, tall, slim, and sparse tree would make good timber for building and the long branches would make good firewood for the winter."

So, they pulled out their axes and chopped the second tree down.

Up to the Church

Two Christians went up to the church to pray.

The first Christian went to the front of the church and, looking up toward heaven, said, "Thank you, God, for not making me like other Christians. I pray from the heart, I speak in tongues, and I profess Jesus Christ as my personal savior."

The second Christian knelt in the last pew with head down and prayed, "I'm sorry, Lord, I wish I was better at this faith thing. But, you see I work long hours, I have kids to raise, bills to pay—what I need is your strength and love."

You're So Defensive

For someone who is free

You're awfully defensive.

Old Age

If you want
people to love you when you're old
you better do more than just tolerate them
while you're young.

A Gift

A gift not worth giving is usually wrapped very nicely.

The Ham

I once heard a story about a little girl who used to watch her mother prepare ham for dinner. In preparing the ham, the mother always cut off two inches from both sides of the ham.

The girl asked her mother one day, "Mom, why do you cut two inches off the sides of the ham before you place the ham in the pan and then in the oven?"

"Well, you see," said the mother, "I learned this trick from your grandmother—I used to watch her and that is what she used to do before she put the ham in the pan and then in the oven."

"I see," said the little girl, "but why?"

The mother thought and said, "I think it's because it makes the ham taste different—it gives it a distinctive taste."

One day the little girl was at her grandmother's house and they were both in the kitchen preparing ham for dinner. The little girl watched her grandmother cut two inches off the side of the ham just like her mother.

The little girl asked her grandmother, "Grandma, why do you cut two inches off the sides of the ham before you place it in the pan and then in the oven?"

"Well, you see," said the grandmother, "I learned this trick from my mother—this is what she used to do before she put the ham in the pan and then in the oven."

"I see," said the little girl, "but why?"

The grandmother thought and said, "I think it's because it allows the heat to go all the way through the ham while it's cooking."

It so happened, not too long after, the little girl was at her great grandmother's house and she was in the kitchen watching her great grandmother preparing a ham for dinner. Her great grandmother cut two inches off the side of the ham, placed the ham in the pan, and then placed the pan in the oven.

The little girl then asked her great grandmother, "Granny, why do you cut two inches off the sides of the ham before you place it in the pan and then in the oven?"

"Well, you see," said the great grandmother, "If I don't cut two inches off both sides of the ham I will never be able to fit the ham into my pan."

The Wounded Child

The Wounded Child sinks with tears behind the other forgotten refuse outside. His eyes are heavy and his heart is empty—all he feels is fear—so he must hide. If he speaks, if he stands, will he be heard or seen? Out of fear of rejection he stays slouched down but he is grounded with the earth.

At the fence of the soul stands a man—content with his success as he looks over his shoulder at the glory he has made for himself. Yet, he stands at the fence looking into the darkness that he knows possesses something he needs to hold. He calls out—no response. Voices from within the house call him back to his world, but he struggles, he refuses to go back into the house just yet. He must find what he is lacking. He stands and ponders the darkness—he quiets the noises within him and he begins to hear a whine—a sigh. Soft, yet distinct—there's something out there in the darkness. He calls out again—the sound of silence returns.

He wanders back into the house—the wounded child slouches closer to the ground and is almost absorbed by the grass. They both sleep—content in their own worlds and yet afraid and curious of the other they don't know how to enter or attain.

In the morning, the man brings a saw, a hinge, and a latch. He dismantles part of the fence and makes a gate. The gate he builds swings in two directions and can be locked in position only if latched. He leaves the latch open. Standing by the gate he peers again into the darkness—he wonders what calls to him to go—he wants to call out, but he thinks his volume may frighten away what's out there. He opens the gate and walks out.

He immediately encounters weeds, high grass, mud, and muck. "How can anything live out here?" he thinks. Slowly and carefully he treads—he hears the whine and the sigh again and the farther he goes the thicker the weeds, the grass, the mud, and the muck. He stumbles upon a disregarded memory and when he looks down to pick it up he begins to see an array of children's toys tossed about, ruined and beaten by weather and neglect.

As he picks up a stuffed bear, he notices the mouth has been ripped off and its fur has been frayed. The longer he gazes at it, the easier he recognizes it as his own. The child is watching from a distance. This bear was taken away from him because he was told he was too old to play with such toys. He was hurt and confused and he couldn't speak—no one ever knew how much that bear meant to him. Then, the man starts to cry as he recalls the painful memory.

Off to the left, turned on its side, is his bike. Once green, now faded rusty yellow. The pedals are missing and the tires flat. He remembers how he and his friends would ride around for hours feeling so free. When the bike broke he asked that it be fixed—it never was. Would he ever feel free like that again, he wonders.

He starts to pick up clothing and records that he used to have; that one day he found missing from his room and nothing was ever said. And yet, he realizes he lost track of all these things as he grew older because what other people wanted him to be was more important. But now, the longer he stands and looks around the more he notices the more he remembers things from his childhood that have been discarded and forgotten: a card he once made, a box filled with old pictures, and gifts lying out by the trash.

The man goes around with the box and collects all the items he can find. He holds them to his heart and feels stronger, at least his memory is coming back. After he collects all the discarded pieces of his childhood he goes back through the gate and into his house and closes the door. He had not seen the child in the darkness. He goes through each item one at a time—he sees their broken pieces, their dirty parts, their ripped edges, and yet, he remembers and can still see their beauty through their ugliness.

When he finishes, he stands at the window and looks out over the fence. The child can see him in the distance through the darkness. The man then says to the darkness, "Tomorrow I will search again…"

A Skeleton in the Attic

Once Upon A Time, there was a big house that had a skeleton in the attic. The family that lived there was very frightened by this skeleton so they insisted that no one in the family should ever go up to the attic. And yet, it so happened that one day the little boy who lived in the house, and who was very curious by nature, secretly made his way up to the attic. When he got to the attic and opened the door he immediately saw the skeleton sitting in the corner of the attic. He was scared at the sight of this ugly skeleton, but he entered the attic and sat far away from the skeleton and just looked at it for a while. For a whole year the little boy would sneak up to the attic and would just sit on the floor and look upon the skeleton from a distance.

When a year had passed, he realized that he was no longer really scared by the skeleton's presence, so he attempted to get closer to it. He moved right next to it and for some reason he started to talk to it. The more he talked with it the more comfortable he felt being close to it. Of course, the skeleton didn't talk back, but the boy just pretended. He would tell the skeleton all the things he was afraid of and even how he was afraid of coming to the attic. After about a year, the boy, in the midst of one of his conversations with the skeleton, just reached out and touched it.

When he touched its coarse bone, he startled himself because he felt how cold and hard the skeleton was. But what was even more startling was the fact that the skeleton started to speak back to the boy. The skeleton told the boy not to be afraid, and he thanked the boy for allowing him to talk by touching him.

"For two years," the skeleton said, "I have waited to speak, and your simple touch has unlocked my lips. Now, when you come back tomorrow we can both talk."

So, for a whole year the two of them would talk about life, and death. The boy would ask the skeleton what it was like to be treated so badly by people. He asked the skeleton why people were so afraid of him.

The skeleton said, "People are not comfortable talking to things that look strange, ugly, or remind them of painful things. People are scared of me because I remind them of death."

The boy however was very happy to have made a new friend with this skeleton, and he thought, perhaps, if he put clothes on the skeleton it would feel better about itself.

So the boy brought up clothes to the attic and he picked the skeleton up off the floor—but when he embraced the skeleton with his arms the skeleton all of a sudden started to walk by himself.

The skeleton was so happy and said, "Oh, thank you so much for clothing me with your embrace. All I needed was your arms around me to give me strength. Now I can walk."

So, for another year the skeleton and the boy would walk around the attic, talk, and laugh. The boy grew to love the skeleton and the skeleton was very grateful to the boy for all the gifts of life he had given it. One day, as they were hopping around the attic, the skeleton tripped over a trunk that was in the center of the room. It fell over and landed very hard. Its legs were shattered and its skull was cracked—the skeleton was now unable to walk and almost unable to speak. The boy ran over to the skeleton and picked it up, brought it over to the windowsill, and laid it out, trying to make it comfortable.

The skeleton looked at the boy and said, "It looks like I will have to go back to being a mute-and-still skeleton again. But, before I go back, I just want to thank you for all the gifts of life you have given me."

The boy started to cry and told the skeleton he didn't want him to die or stop being his friend. The boy told the skeleton that he loved him as a real person and then he leaned over and kissed the skeleton on the crack of the forehead. As soon as the boy's lips touched the skull, the skeleton turned into a fleshy person.

The boy couldn't believe his eyes and said, "You are a real person—now you'll be alright."

"No," said the skeleton, "I will soon be gone—I will disappear—but your love and kiss has given me, in my final minutes, the gift of being a real person. Thank you very much. When you leave here today, I will go away and you will never see me again, but you must remember this moment, so, when you meet other skeletons you will not be afraid to sit with them, talk with them, touch them, embrace them, and kiss them. It is because of your love that you have been able to conquer your fear of skeletons, and at the same time your love has given me the life of a real person—even though now I must die.

"Look at me now, but remember me as I once was: a skeleton you found in the attic."

Into the Woods…

Once Upon A Time, there was a boy who lived in a very happy family near the edge of the woods. One day, as he was gathering wood in the forest, a dragon came, set fire to his cottage, and killed his parents who were inside. Upon returning home, instead of being greeted by a kiss from his mother, the boy was greeted by the smoke of smoldering ashes. Realizing that all he loved was now gone, the boy sank to his knees and cried.

Just then, the dragon reappeared in the distance. So, taken by fear, the boy rose from the ground and with all his strength ran for his life in search of a place to hide. The boy ran and ran until he found himself far into the woods and lost. When the immediate threat of the dragon had disappeared, the boy began to walk cautiously, turning around at every strange sound. And as night began to cast its blanket of darkness over everything in the woods, the boy became even more frightened. There he was, walking aimlessly in the woods, still without shelter, now cold and hungry. But what haunted the boy most of all was that he knew he was alone—alone and lost somewhere deep within the woods.

Just when his feet could carry him no more, and his body was thoroughly penetrated by the cold night air, he found himself standing in front of a pair of large wooden doors. As he looked up past the doors, he couldn't believe his eyes, for stretching straight up into the night sky was what looked like an abandoned tower. Delighted by his find, he quickly entered the dark tower, and swiftly locked himself behind its doors; then, he eagerly climbed up to the top of the tower, for he knew he would be safe there. Once at the top, he cautiously made his way to the window and looked out at the dark woods below. With all signs of danger now securely locked outside, he stretched himself out across the cold stone floor, closed his eyes and slept.

Now, also living in the tower was a crafty old witch. She had secretly watched the boy enter the tower, and this unexpected intrusion pleased her greatly. Once the boy was fast asleep, she went over to him and quietly whispered spells into his ears.

"Don't be afraid anymore. I will protect you, my son. As long as you stay with me in this tower no dragon will ever devour you. The woods, my boy, are cruel; but I am kind—believe me, my boy. Now sleep, my son, sleep. And when you wake, you'll be safe—I will take care of you forever."

Yes, the crafty old witch did take care of the boy for many years and the boy did feel very safe in the tower. Yet, in spite of his safety, the boy was becoming more and more unhappy because he felt trapped by the same tower that once sheltered him. And whenever the boy tried to convey this feeling to the witch, she would only remind him about the dragon and how her tower had saved him from wandering aimlessly in the cold dark woods; and these words, like the earlier spell, would silence his urges to leave.

On one occasion, however, the boy and the witch got into a very heated argument about his ability to care for himself in the woods. So, outraged by the boy's stubbornness on the matter, the witch threatened to leave him for good if he ever so much as set foot out of the tower. And with her threat, she disappeared for a long time leaving the boy alone and frightened in the tower.

It came to pass that one day, as he sat alone in the tower afraid that his witch would never return, the boy saw from his window a young man with a sword in hand sitting on a stump below the tower and looking very sad.

The boy called out to the man, "*What's the matter, sir? You look so troubled.*"

The young man replied, "*My love has been consumed by a dragon, and I have failed in my attempt to save her.*"

The boy, wanting to hear more of the story, continued by saying, "*Please, sir, start from the beginning so I can hear all of your sad tale.*"

"*I would be glad to, my boy,*" said the man. "*But why don't you first come down from that ridiculous tower, so I can speak to you in person and save my voice from losing its quality? It would be much easier for me to talk to you directly than to yell up to your window.*"

The possibility of leaving the tower had never occurred to the boy, and as he thought about it, he replied, "*But I can't, I'm locked in.*"

"*Who has the key?*" the young man asked.

"Yes, who has the key?" the boy thought. Then he remembered, "*I do! I have the key!*" The boy shouted triumphantly. "*I locked myself in here in the first place.*" The boy then ran down the steps with an energy he had forgotten he possessed. He opened the doors to the tower and slowly stepped out into the woods for the first time in years—and it was all so mysteriously new.

The boy greeted the young man with a kiss, turned around and looked at the doors now opened, and sat next to the young man on the stump and said, "*Please, sir, go on and tell me your story from the very beginning—I am eager to hear it.*"

The young man then handed his sword to the boy, stood up, and began to recount his story in detail.

"*The sword you now hold is cursed. My grandfather used to blame the sword for all the trials that the men in our family were forced to endure. And ever since I remember misfortune, hunger, and death were frequent visitors to the men in our family.*

"'*Why not dispose of the sword?' I know you're thinking. Well, I asked my father the same question, and he said to me that one day I would understand. 'The sword,' he said, 'will cast a spell on you as it has on me and the other men in our family before me—you can't dispose of this sword because it claims you.'*

"'How absurd,' I thought, Yet, hardly a week had passed that, on my seventeenth birthday, I came home from the blacksmith's barn to find my house, my parents, and the farm destroyed by an enraged dragon. Standing in the midst of the ashes and the smoke of my past, I realized that there was nothing left for me there. I wept for my parents and for the memories that had burned, and went off to sit under the shade of a tree my grandfather had planted about a hundred yards away from the house.

"As I leaned against the tree, I noticed that the dirt beneath my feet had been freshly dug. So, I reached into the ground to see what treasure the earth had laid waiting for me. And, lo and behold, what did I find? The only thing of value that had not been destroyed—the cursed sword. My father must have hidden it under the tree to protect it from the dragon. It is the very sword you're now holding.

"After I dug the sword up from the ground, a strange feeling came over me, as though I were

responsible for it in some way. As I examined the sword carefully, I noticed the name of the Kingdom of Ithaca with the royal crest engraved, as you can see, on the steel. The sword had most likely belonged to a king. My grandfather must have stolen it, or found it, and that's why the men in our family have been cursed ever since. My journey, as far as I can see, is to travel to Ithaca and return the sword to its rightful owner before any more misfortune befalls me or my sons to be."

The boy interrupted the young man and asked, "*But what about your love who was consumed by the dragon?*"

"*Oh yes,*" said the young man. "*Once I had possession of the sword, I knew the dragon would pursue me, so into the woods I ran for safety. Dragons will not enter the woods because they cannot fly in the forest. In my haste to flee, I forgot about Evelynne, my love. After two days in the woods, I returned to the village to bid her farewell before I set out on my journey, but the dragon in his outrage for not finding the sword had burned the whole village to the ground, and with it my love.*

"*Now, all that I possess is the sword—a sword that is truly cursed, and whose curse will not be removed until it is safely in the hands of its rightful owner. This, I see, is my quest, for there's nothing else to keep me from making this journey.*

"*It was at this point that I stumbled onto this stump, where I could sit and rest. I heard a voice from above, and it was you. And that, dear boy, is my tale. I thank you for giving me an ear to tell it.*"

The boy quickly responded, "*I am the one who is honored. For years I have been locked in that tower afraid to leave—afraid to leave for the very same reason you must journey through the woods to return the cursed sword, the hostile dragon. You see, a dragon also has killed my family and is pursuing me. For what reason I do not know, but I have found safety from the cruel, dark woods in the tower.*"

The young man answered, "*Yes, the woods are dark and cruel, but there are also many magnificent creatures and persons in the woods. One must wander and journey for a while in order to see these treasures, and if one wants to be true to one's quest. Would you like to journey with me—into the woods?*"

"*But I am afraid,*" the boy cautiously said.

The man replied, "*I understand your fear, but now you have my sword in hand. It will protect us from any animals, thieves, and danger we might encounter; and it will also serve as the means to provide food. Please, come with me. I can use a companion and I will show you how to use this sword. Besides, it is easier to walk into the woods by two than it is all alone.*"

The boy stood silent for a moment. He turned and looked at the tower. The doors were still open, and he knew it was safe inside. This new journey excited the boy, and yet it also scared him. But when the boy looked at the sword and embraced its power, it seemed that the sword was claiming him and giving him life. So, he faced the young man and, filled with courage, said, "*Yes, I will journey with you into the woods.*"

The journey excited the boy in a way that sent life coursing through every fiber of his body. He began to feel that "the boy" who had earlier locked himself in the tower was now on the way to becoming a man—and somehow he knew that it would be in the woods that this transformation to manhood would take place. And maybe the dragons, the witches, and anything else he might encounter in the woods were all part of his journey—a journey that possessed a treasure he needed to discover.

As soon as he had agreed to leave, the doors to the tower slammed shut and from the window the boy heard the witch scream, "*If you go too far into the woods you shall never return as you are. Heed my warning or you shall pay dearly for abandoning your tower!*"

Nevertheless, the boy just covered his ears, held tight to the sword, and walked with his new companion straight *into the wood…*

I Want to Fly

Once Upon A Time, on a little farm out in the woods, there was born a little bird who cracked out of his shell before the time his mother expected, so she had flown from the nest to find some food for her soon-to-be-new infant to eat.

Well, when the little bird popped out of the shell, he was very curious about where he was and started to look around with much intensity.

The Great Tree who was good friends with the mother bird said to the little bird, "Now, you be careful. You're very small and your mother's not here to care for you."

But the little bird wandered over to the side of the nest and began to peer over the side and see the world below. He marveled at all that was around him for it was all so new—and he was curious about it. The Great Tree again warned him not to bend too far, but it was too late. No sooner had the Great Tree warned him then the little bird fell right over the side of the nest and right down onto the back of a passing turtle.

The turtle was startled by this sudden crash on his back and asked the Great Tree, "What happened? What fell on me from your great branches?"

The Great Tree responded, "The little bird from the nest has fallen from his home."

So, the turtle waited patiently for the little bird to come to and when he did he asked the turtle, "What happened? How did I get down here?"

"You fell from the Great Tree," the turtle replied.

"Well, how can I go back?" asked the little bird.

The turtle said, "The only way for you to get back to your nest is to fly. Do you know how to fly?"

The little bird answered, "No, I don't know how to fly. Now, I guess, I'll never get back home. I'm stuck down here forever."

The turtle thought for a few seconds and said, "Wait a minute. Why don't we go around and ask the other farm animals, maybe they can help you learn how to fly?"

So the turtle slowly walked the little bird over to Mr. Donkey who was carrying a bundle of firewood on his back.

The turtle interrupted Mr. Donkey and said, "Pardon me, Mr. Donkey, but this little friend is very sad because he can't fly and he'd be very happy if you could help him learn how to fly."

Mr. Donkey laughed, saying, "You're not serious, are you? What do you need to fly for? Look at me, I'm on the ground and I work all day carrying these burdens for my master. I'm obedient and loyal, I work hard and I get plenty of hay. I don't fly, and I'm happy on the ground. What do you need to fly for?"

The little bird responded, "Because, I want to go home."

But seeing that they were getting nowhere with Mr. Donkey, the turtle slowly walked the little bird over to Mr. Dog who was wagging his tail cheerfully.

"Pardon me, Mr. Dog," said the turtle, "but this little friend of mine is very sad because he can't fly, and he'd be very happy if you could help him learn how to fly."

Mr. Dog howled when he heard this and said, "You're not serious are you? What do you need to fly for? Look at me, I'm on the ground and I wag my tail, I let my master stroke my back, I accompany him wherever he wants me to go, and I please my master very much. I'm obedient and cheerful and I play all day. I don't fly, and I'm happy on the ground. What do you need to fly for?"

The little bird responded, "Because, I want to go home."

But just like the donkey, they saw they were getting nowhere with Mr. Dog, so the turtle slowly made his way over to Mrs. Hen who was busy laying eggs.

"Pardon me Mrs. Hen," said the turtle, "but this little friend of mine is very sad because he can't fly, and he'd be very happy if you could help him learn how to fly."

Mrs. Hen cackled when she heard this and said, "You're not serious are you? What do you need to fly for? Look at me, I'm on the ground and I can sit in my pen all day long without a worry in the world. I just lay eggs for my master and he gives me plenty of seeds to eat. I'm obedient and productive and you see I don't fly. I'm happy on the ground. What do you need to fly for?"

The little bird responded, "Because, I want to go home."

But just like with Mr. Donkey and Mr. Dog, they saw they were getting nowhere with Mrs. Hen, so the turtle slowly made his way back over to the Great Tree.

"So, Little Bird," asked the Great Tree, "did you find out how to fly?"

"No," responded the bird sadly. "None of the other farm animals would help me."

"Well," said the Great Tree, "perhaps I can help you. But first, let me ask you, why do you want to fly?"

The little bird thought how silly the question was and said, "You know why I need to fly—because I want to go home."

"I see, but is that the only reason for which you want to fly—just to come back up here? What good is flying if you are only stuck in some other place?"

"I see," said the little bird, "You're right, I really want to fly so I can be free. I don't want to be stuck here on the ground forever, or even up there in the nest. I want to be free to fly—then I will be happy."

"Very Good!" said the Great Tree. "Now, you are ready to learn how to fly."

"But, how can you—A Great Tree—show me—a little bird—how to fly?" asked the little bird.

"I know many things—and you must trust my wisdom." said the Great Tree. "Now do as I instruct. First extend out your wings like my branches, as far as they can go."

The little bird extended his wings.

"Good! Now, wave your wings up and down like my branches wave in when the breeze hits them."

The little bird started to wave his wings back and forth.

"Good!" said the Great Tree.

But the little bird, seeing he was not moving said, "But I'm not flying. I thought you said you would teach me how to fly."

"I will." answered back the Great Tree. "But now you must do one more thing."

And as the Great Tree said this, he bent down and picked up the little bird and placed him back in the nest from which he fell and said, "Now, you are home. And if you really want to fly you must jump from your nest and do what I have instructed."

The little bird was terrified, "But, I am afraid." he said.

"Of course you are afraid," said the Great Tree, "because you know that once before you fell from the nest. Now, my little bird, you must jump and trust that you will fly if you do what will come naturally to you."

So, the little bird walked over to the edge of the nest and, climbing on the side, jumped with all the courage he could muster. He opened his wings and waved them like the Great Tree had told him—and before he knew it, he was gliding and then he was flying up—up into the air—he was free at last and it felt very natural.

Now that the little bird could fly, he flew over to the Mr. Donkey, Mr. Dog, and Mrs. Hen to show them that he could fly, but they just snorted, growled, and cackled at him because they were busy pleasing their master.

Finally, the little bird flew over to the Great Tree and thanked him for his wisdom that inspired his ability to fly and asked the Great Tree, "How come you know so much about flight and being free when you are always in the same place all the time?"

The Great Tree humbly bowed its branches and said,

"Oh, I may be in the same place all the time—but I am grounded here. My roots go deep into the earth and they are free to move where the sources of life are to be found—just like your nest is to you—and no one can take that away. I have branches that extend as far as they want to go just like your wings and no one can limit them or stop them from waving in the breeze. My trunk grows high up into the sky just like you are able to fly into the sky and no one can keep it down. You see, when we're doing what comes naturally, we become masters of our own flight and we can truly be free. Now fly, little bird, fly and be free."

Death Is Life

Death

The only motivating force to life. And yet people live as though they are dying.

How can life be a celebration of what it really is unless the absence of it is really faced?

Death forces me to live…
to see the smiles I casually ignore, so I don't have to enter into another relationship.

Death challenges me to feel…
and not hide my purest most vulnerable self.

Death wants me to see…
what expectant eyes can't: the moment.

Death wants me to cry…
the tears that apathy has dried.

Death is not morbid—she is inviting me to live. Now!

People are here! Family is here! Life is here!

When death takes my hand, she will ask me for my gift and I want to give "my life."

Death sits and waits in the corner almost indiscreetly. Every now and then she sees me and calls me to live.

"You frighten me! You're ugly! You're mean!" I say.

"No, I'm wise. I can be your friend and teacher." Death responds, "Don't you see, I am Life."

Doors

Once Upon A Time, there was a boy who never left his room because it provided him with everything he ever needed. His room was very large and was filled with many things: toys, clothes, food, books. Anything the boy needed, he would eventually find in his room. The boy thought he was happy, so he spent many hours, days, and years preoccupied with all the things in his room.

Whenever he got curious and approached the door, he would see the words scratched on the door post, "Why go looking anywhere else—just ask for what you need and the room will provide it." So, everything he asked for he found. Yet, with all these things, the boy thought that there must be something outside his door that his room could not provide.

So, he went to his door, at first he thought it would be locked, but it wasn't. Then, he read the words on the post, but he ignored them and walked out into the hall. The hall was dark, so he went back to his room and found an old flashlight and started out again. With his flashlight in hand, the boy could see that the hall had three closed doors. He wondered if these rooms were safe, he knew he would have to find out for himself.

When the boy opened the first door a voice screamed from inside. When he looked in, however, there was no one to be found.

The boy called out and asked, "Who is in here?"

The voice replied, "I am. Now, who are you?"

The boy answered, "I am the boy down the hall."

"Oh, you are the boy who has everything he needs." said the voice. "Why did you come here? I have nothing but a voice."

"Well, maybe we can speak together," the boy offered. "For I don't have anyone to talk with."

"Yes," agreed the voice.

So, the boy and the voice started to talk. Since the door of the voice was now open the voice was able to follow the boy to his room and they continued to talk and talk all night long.

The next day, the voice and the boy went to the next closed door in the hall and when they opened it they found a boy doll sitting in a chair. The doll was as big as the boy but it was just a doll, so the voice said, "Why don't I become the voice of the doll then you will have someone to look at when we talk?"

The boy was happy with this new change because now he seemed to have a companion.

The boy sat the doll in his chair and talked to him all night long. The next day the boy asked the doll-voice to go with him to the last door.

"No!" exclaimed the doll-voice, and it began to cry real tears.

"Why?" asked the boy.

"Because once you see what's in there you will not need us anymore." the doll-voice explained.

"Well, what's in there?" asked the boy.

The doll-voice would not answer, so the boy left his room headed straight for the third door carrying the doll-voice in his arms.

"Please don't go inside," pleaded the doll-voice, "everything you need is out here and in your room." But the boy dropped the doll-voice on the floor and opened the third door.

When he stepped inside the room all he saw was what looked like a large wall painting. And, as he approached the large wall-painting he got frightened by it because it began to move. The boy ran out of the room and went to pick up the doll-voice but it was gone. He tried to open the doors where he had found them but they were now locked. He made his way back to his room, closed the door, and read the words, "Why go looking anywhere else, just ask for what you need and the room will provide it." He asked for the doll-voice to come back. His attempt was in vain, for his room could not provide friendship. He knew now that the promise of the room was a lie, so he went back to the third door again to see who was in that wall-painting.

When he entered the room, he went right up to the wall-painting. As he raised his hand to touch who was inside, the person in the wall-painting raised his hand to touch the boy.

When the two hands touched, the boy said, "Hey, you, trapped behind this glass. Who are you?"

The wall painting replied, "I am you."

The boy responded, "That's me?" pointing to the figure in the glass. "You're me?"

"Yes!" said the wall-painting.

"How come you are or I am, trapped behind that glass?" asked the boy.

"Well, aren't you trapped within your room?" said the wall-painting

"Yes, I guess I am, or at least I was until today," said the boy. "How can I, or we, get out of our traps?"

The wall-painting then said, "Take down my picture from the wall, and behind me you will see another door that will free the both of us. Go on, open the door and step outside. I'll be with you—but you must go first."

So the boy stepped outside into the world for the first time in his life, the image and voice then left the wall-painting and entered into the boy's heart. And, at that moment, the boy heard his heart say, "Now, I am with you. We no longer need to stay here. Let us move on and find more doors to open."

Spite Myself

There once was a man who, when walking on a path in the middle of the village, stumbled over a stone on his way home one night. So angry at the stone in his way, the man decided never to take that path ever again. So instead, whenever the man traveled to or from the village, he would take the long way around the village. When walking with friends, the man insisted they avoid the path with the stone in the middle of the village and go with him because he refused to go that way. When his friends questioned him about this, the man would get angry and go his own way leaving many of his friends behind.

It so happened that one day the man saw a little boy crying. The man asked the boy what was the matter and it turned out that the little boy had tripped over the same stone on the path in the middle of the village. The man then said to the boy, "You should do what I do and take the long way around the village and avoid the stone altogether."

The boy wiped his eyes and said, "Why should I spite myself and change my path over one small stone when it's easier to step around it now that I know it's there. Besides, there are many beautiful things on this path in the middle of the village, namely my friends."

Love's Will

Once Upon A Time, there was a young man who was confused about how to love. Oh, he tried but everyone he met he soon fell out of love with because they either were too possessive or didn't love him back. What was he to do?

The young man thought, "Is it worth loving someone if it always ends as a lonely experience?"

In spite of his pessimism, he met a wonderful person and fell in love. The two became very close almost immediately. The young man was taken in by this new love—heart and all. Needless to say, the young man was not prepared when the distance set in and withdrawal came along. It looked like the young man was going to be alone again. The young man was terribly sad and thought, "Is it worth loving someone if it always ends as a lonely experience?"

The young man decided to take a walk in the woods and to seriously think about his sad experience of love. The young man came across a large stone so he sat upon it and finally, unable to hold back any longer, he let the tears of sorrow fill his eyes.

It was just at this point that an old white-haired man passed the young man. The old white-haired man stopped and asked the young man on the stone why he was crying. (But, you see, the old white-haired man already knew because he recognized tears of lost love.)

After listening to the young man's story, the old white-haired man sat down on the ground next to the stone and said, "Go on, my son. Cry good and hard. Let the tears of childhood love wash you clean and water your growth."

When the young man's tears surrendered, the old man said, "Now, listen, young man. Love is not just what you want it to be. Love doesn't measure the other person or should it be used as a tool to measure you. Now, do you really love this person?"

"Yes." said the young man.

"Did you tell this person?" asked the old white-haired man.

"Yes," responded the young man. "But my love doesn't love me back."

The old white-haired man looked into the young man's eyes and said, "Then love and let go. You know you cannot demand love in return— if so, then it's not love, is it?"

"Why is it that my head hears you, but my heart can't change the way it feels?" asked the young man.

"Because," said the old white-haired man, "you must learn how to love not only with the heart of feelings but with the heart of will."

Buttons

Once Upon A Time, a man was given a button by a mysterious stranger. The button was no larger or smaller than an ordinary button, yet, there was something distinct about this button—it was made of glass and therefore it was very fragile to handle. Before the stranger departed, he told the man that the button possessed the magical power of love.

As the man held the button in his hand and looked at it, a feeling of immense love and tranquility came over him. He couldn't explain the sensation for he had never experienced such depth of feeling before. Whenever he put the button down or separated himself from it for a while, the wonderful feeling left and he became frustrated and nervous.

It didn't take the man long to realize that the button did actually possess magical powers, so he proceeded to sew the button onto his shirt so he would never have to be without this feeling.

First, the man tried to sew the button to the collar of his shirt, but the needle wouldn't penetrate through the holes in the button. "How strange," the man thought. Then he tried to sew the button down the center of the shirt, but this too was in vain.

"What is going on here?" the man blurted out, as though he was asking the button.

The button answered back, "Just what are you trying to do?"

The man was surprised at this, but he answered nevertheless, "I'm trying to sew you onto my shirt, so I will always feel this tremendous feeling I have when I'm with you."

"Oh, then you must sew me on the inside of your shirt pocket." replied the button.

Not fully understanding this, the man sewed the button onto the inside of his shirt pocket, and as he stitched through the two holes on the button he pricked his finger with each stitch. The pain hurt so bad the man began to cry and bleed, so he asked the button, "If you're supposed to make me feel good, why are you causing me so much pain?"

The button said, "To truly possess my power means to be open to this pain."

"I don't understand, open to what pain?" the man questioned further.

"The pain of joy and the pain of sorrow." was the button's reply.

The man came back, "But, I just want the good feeling your power gives."

"No!" the button said sharply, "The power to feel good is only part of my power of love, and if you truly want my power always, you must also take the pain that goes with the joy and the pain that will come with the sorrow of loving."

The man didn't quite understand all this—he just wanted the button sewed on. When he finished stitching the button onto his shirt pocket, his pocket mysteriously closed shut. Although the man tried and tried to reopen the pocket, the button would not unfasten.

Finally, the man asked the button, "Why is it I can't open my pocket?"

"Your pocket is not different from your heart." was all the button would say.

"What?" cried the man.

There was no explanation, so he asked, "What good is having a pocket if it doesn't open to hold something special?"

The button responded, "And what good is having a heart if it doesn't open to hold someone special?"

Too confused to argue further, the man put his shirt on. Not long after, he realized that he didn't have that wonderful feeling the button promised to give.

The man asked, "Hey, if you belong to me now, why don't I feel your power?"

After a short pause, the button replied.

"It's not me—a button in your pocket that can give you this power or feeling—it's your heart." said the button. "You wanted so badly to have love in your life that you thought I actually gave it to you, but it was really your own heart's desire to be loved that created those feelings. Then, when your heart was finally open to feel love and you felt some pain come in, you closed your heart to stop the pain but with it you also stopped the joy. Don't you see, you possess this power already, but you will never feel love again until you allow someone to touch your heart and open its way out of you. Only when this happens will your pocket be opened once again—now, go—and you shall not hear from me again until that day."

So off the man went into life. When he found the person who touched his heart and opened his feelings to love, his pocket button opened immediately and said, "You've found love at last, I see."

The man, overcome with much joy, said, "Yes, and I didn't realize love was more than just good feelings."

"Well what have you learned then?" asked the button.

The man thought for a minute and said.

"Well, as carefully as I stitched you onto my shirt, I learned I had to carefully sew my love. When I found the right person with whom I wanted my love to grow, it was the cause of great joy but soon after there was pain and sorrow—I learned that all growth in love comes at a cost. I thank you, my dear button, for teaching me how to open my heart to love and not be afraid of the pain that comes with joy and sorrow that love brings with it."

"Now, be still," said the button. "Trust this love you have found—let its power come alive in your heart and make you happy. But you must do one more thing for me."

"What is that?" asked the man.

The button paused and then said, "Pass me onto another stranger in the same way you received me. As a button, I must be about the business of opening hearts that are closed."

Knock

Once Upon A Time, there was a little boy named Adam who heard a knock on his door, and since he was the only one home he answered the door. Upon opening the door, Adam was surprised to see that there was no one there. He stepped out of the house to look into the street and as he walked away from the door it slammed closed behind him.

Unfortunately, Adam did not have a key for the door so he sat down outside the door and waited. A short time had passed, and a boy not much older than himself passed by. Adam asked the boy if he was the one that knocked on the door.

The boy responded, "No, it wasn't me, but perhaps the one who knocked on the door is out here somewhere. Why don't you look for him?"

"No!" Adam said. "I must sit here and wait for someone to open the door."

The little boy, now looking at the house a little closer, realized that he once lived there. And he told Adam about a secret passage he had made in the back of the house that would allow him to get back in the house.

So, Adam followed the little boy to the back of the house, through the small passage, and back into the house. Adam was very pleased but when he went to thank the boy, the boy disappeared. Adam was alone.

Years passed and Adam was now much older. Just like before he heard a knock on his door, and since he was the only one home he went to answer it. Upon opening the door, Adam was once again surprised to see that there was no one there.

Just like before, he stepped out of the house to look into the street, and as he walked away from the door it slammed closed behind him. And since Adam did not have a key he was locked outside again. So, like before, he sat down outside the door and waited. A short time had passed when a beautiful woman walked by him.

Adam asked the beautiful woman if she was the one who had knocked on his door.

She responded, "No, I'm sorry, I'm not the one you're looking for, but perhaps the one who knocked is out here. Why don't you go look for him."

"No!" responded Adam, "I must sit here and wait for someone to open the door."

"Well, I do not have the key for this door," said the woman, "But I used to live here and I know of a secret passage on the side of the house. Come with me and I will show you."

So, Adam followed the woman to the side of the house where there was painted a huge mural and hidden very shrewdly in the mural was a door. Adam entered the secret door after the woman, but as he stepped foot in the house, the beautiful woman disappeared. Adam was alone again.

Many years passed and Adam was now an adult. His parents were both dead so he lived alone in his house. Just like before, he heard a knock on his door, and since he was alone, he went to answer the door. Upon opening the door, Adam wasn't surprised to see that there was no one there because he remembered the other times.

So, just like before, he stepped out of the house to look into the street and he knew that as he walked away from the door it would slam closed behind him. But this time he wasn't worried that he had no key, so he just sat down outside the door and waited, for he knew someone would eventually approach and let him back into his house.

Sure enough, in just a short time an old man walked by the house. Adam asked him if he had knocked on the door.

The old man responded, "No." Adam was not surprised. The old man continued, "I'm sorry I am not the one you are looking for—but perhaps the one who knocked is out here somewhere—why don't you go look for him?"

"No!" said Adam. "Besides, I bet you used to live here many years ago and you know a secret passage."

"Yes," said the old man. "I did live here many years ago, but there is no secret passage for you to enter besides the front door and I do not have the key."

Adam quickly added, "But what about the small passage in the back of the house?"

"Too small for either of us to enter now," said the old man. "Besides it is no longer, dirt and rock now occupy the passage that was once clear."

Then Adam immediately said, "Well, what about the secret door on the side of the house that is hidden in the mural?"

"Oh, yes," said the old man. "I remember that door. But if you look now, the mural has faded away because of neglect and sunlight—I'm sorry to say this, but the door no longer exists. The only way you can enter this house is through this door, and since I don't have the key I can not help you."

"What am I to do?" asked Adam. "Every time I heard a knock I answered the door—and every time I was locked out of my house, there was always someone who passed by and let me in."

"Yes, but never through the front door. The time has come, Adam," said the old man, "that you find the one who has been knocking on your door. When you find him you will have found the key—and to possess the key means that you can go and come as you please from your house and you will never be locked out of your house again."

The Boy without a Reflection

Once Upon A Time, deep in the forest, there lived a young boy, his beautiful maiden mother, and the maiden's mean and cruel brother. Unfortunately, the beautiful maiden had conceived out of wedlock, so the boy was without a father and as a curse was born without a reflection.

What happened was this: one day, when the maiden was out in the forest kneeling before a large pool washing her clothes, she was surprised to see next to her reflection in the water a handsome woodcutter. She turned around, their eyes met, and they fell instantly in love. For weeks, they would meet out by the pool of water, and one special night they made vows of love and spent the night together.

In the morning, the woodcutter told the beautiful maiden that he had to leave for a while but would return before long and take her as his wife. As a sign of his love, he gave her a gold pin. He told her that only two such pins existed in the whole world, he possessed the other. She kissed her lover good-bye, took the pin, kept it close to her heart, and waited every day by the pool of water for the woodcutter to return.

Time went on and the woodcutter had not returned. By now, the beautiful maiden began to show signs of having spent the night with the woodcutter. Her brother was outraged by this disgrace and beat her for her misconduct and kept the maiden locked up in the cottage till the child was born. The maiden wept bitterly every night till the birth of her son because she thought she would miss the woodcutter's return.

After her son was born, she regained her strength and she took the boy to the pool of water and waited for the woodcutter. However, when she looked into the pool of water and saw her face and how she aged so, she thought, "Surely the woodcutter will not want me now, looking like this." But what was even more frightening was the fact that when she looked at the water with her son in her arms, she noticed that the boy had no reflection in the water. No matter how near the water she held him, he had no reflection. Afraid of this, she brought the boy home and removed all the mirrors from the cottage so that the boy would never know he did not have a reflection.

The years passed and the maiden's brother was getting meaner and meaner toward the growing boy. Every day, however, the woman would go with her son to the pool of water in the forest hoping, not only that the woodcutter would return, but that the boy would somehow gain his reflection. However, on both accounts her hopes were in vain.

It wasn't long after the boy's twelfth birthday that the maiden got very ill and shortly thereafter died, giving to her son, before she died, the pin of the woodcutter. Unfortunately, the boy was left to the maiden's mean and cruel brother to be raised.

The boy's uncle would continue to laugh at him for being without a father, and the uncle would beat the boy for being of no use around the house. Every day, however, the boy would go out to the pool of water in the forest and look into its depths. Since, the boy never knew he didn't have a reflection, he was never bothered by not seeing it, so he just gazed into the water hoping to see whatever it was his mother always longed for but never found.

One day, after being laughed at and beaten by his uncle, the boy went to the pool of water and just as he gazed into it a large black toad came hopping out of the water. The toad landed right on the lap of the young boy and the two just stared at each other for a long time.

Then, to the surprise of the boy, the toad spoke and said, "I want to be your friend. Will you be my friend?"

"I don't know," said the boy, "What is a friend?"

The toad explained how a friend was someone who you could talk with, play with, and learn with.

"Oh," said the boy. "Yes, I would very much like to be your friend."

"Good," said the toad, "now I will teach you how to dance."

So, the toad began to hop around and taught the boy how to dance. For the first time in the boy's life he was filled with joy and laughter and grateful to the pool of water that had given him such a great new friend. The toad asked him to come back everyday, and for a whole year the boy and toad danced in the forest to the pleasure of all the animals, trees and even the wild beasts of the forest. When the boy would dance at home his uncle would laugh at him and beat him, but the boy knew he had a friend in the forest.

A year had passed, when the young boy went into the forest one certain day, and the toad was nowhere to be found. So, the boy went over and looked into the pool of water, to his surprise, however the boy saw a shadowy figure on the surface of the water where he was looking in. He never saw this shadowy figure before and tried to wipe it away with his hands but it wouldn't leave. Just then, the toad came hopping out of the water with a flute in his mouth. The toad then hopped onto the boy's lap, gave him the flute, and said,

"This is a special flute—learn how to play it well."

"I don't know how to play the flute." the boy said. But it was too late, for no sooner had he said this then the toad was gone and back into the water. At that moment, a little golden bird came down from the trees and landed on the boy's shoulder.

The bird said he had watched the boy dance for a whole year and he was so delighted by the boy's dancing that he wanted to be the boy's friend too and show him how to play music like the singing birds. So the bird told the boy to put the flute to his mouth and play the melody he would sing. The bird went onto sing and the boy blew on the flute and out came beautiful music.

For a whole year the boy came back everyday and the bird taught him how to play the music of the forest and her music was the pleasure of all the animals, trees, and even the wild beasts in the forest. When the boy would dance or play his flute at home his uncle would laugh at him and beat him, but the boy knew he could dance and play his flute with his friends in the forest.

Another year had passed when the young boy went into the forest on a certain day and neither the toad nor the bird was anywhere to be found. So, the boy went over and looked into the pool of water as he had done before, and to his surprise not only did she see a shadowy figure over the water but he saw what looked like the form of a mouth on the shadow. He tried to wipe it away but it wouldn't move. He was frightened by this, but no sooner had she seen it then the toad popped out of the water and the bird came down from the trees and they sat on his lap.

The boy was happy to see his friends again. The bird had a feather in his mouth and gave it to the boy.

The bird told the boy, "This is a magic feather, learn how to use it well."

"But I don't know how to use the magic feather," said the boy. "Who will teach me?" But no sooner had he said this then the toad and the bird were gone.

When the boy looked up, he could see that, approaching him from a distance, was a beautiful woman. The beautiful woman was very friendly, and very clever. She told the boy that she had for two years now watched him dance and play his music in the forest. She was delighted by his gift of dance and music that she thought now she would teach him about the gift of capturing images.

"But how can I capture images? I don't understand." said the boy.

"Your magic feather and my knowledge will teach you." So the beautiful woman started to teach the boy how to draw with the magic feather. And the boy began to draw all the things in the forest with such mastery that even the animals, trees and wild beasts in the forest were amazed. After a year of drawing the images of the forest, the beautiful woman then taught the young boy that images could also be captured in words. So she taught the boy how to write and read. For one year more, everyday the boy wrote stories that the beautiful woman taught him how to write.

He wrote beautiful stories about dragons and giants, kings and queens, and far away places he wished one day he could visit. He would tell his stories to all the animals, trees, and wild beasts in the forest and they would listen attentively to every word. When the boy would show his drawings or tell his stories at home, his uncle would laugh at him and beat him, but the boy knew he could dance, play his music, draw, and tell stories in the forest because he had friends there.

Two years had passed since he met the beautiful woman and on a certain day when he went back to the forest, the beautiful woman was nowhere to be found. The boy went back to the pool of water and looked in and this time, to his surprise, he not only saw an outline of a shadowy figure with the form of a mouth, he also saw the form of eyes looking back right at him. He was frightened by this sight and tried to wipe it away but it wouldn't go and just at that point the toad popped out of the water, the bird came down from the tree, and the beautiful woman came out of the forest.

They all sat next to the boy and praised him for his marvelous gifts. The beautiful woman was holding in her hands a large silver sword and she told the boy that he must now learn how to hold the sword, hunt with the sword, and fight with the sword.

"But I do not know how to do these things. Who will teach me?" But, as soon as the boy took hold of the gift the three of them disappeared. There was the boy holding onto the sword, standing by the pool of water, and he didn't know what to do.

As he stood there confused, a strong woodcutter came out of the forest where the beautiful woman had disappeared and greeted him. The woodcutter told the boy that for the past four years he had observed him dance, play his flute, draw his images, and tell his stories—so impressed by this boy's gifts that he wanted to give the boy a gift.

The boy said, "But, I just received this sword and don't know how to use it—perhaps you can show me how."

The woodcutter said, "My instruction, then, will be my gift to you."

Everyday for a year, the woodcutter showed the boy, first how to hold the sword, then how to hunt with the sword, and finally how to fight with the sword. The boy learned very quickly and the woodcutter was pleased with the boy's natural skills. When the boy would show his uncle how he could hold, hunt, and fight with the sword his uncle would laugh at him and beat him, but the boy knew he could dance, play his flute, draw his images, tell his stories, and use his sword in the forest because that was where his real friends were.

Well, many years had passed and the boy was now seventeen. He returned to the forest on a certain day and none of his friends were waiting for him. So he went over to the pool of water, looked in, and to his surprise and fright, he saw the same shadowy figure with a mouth, eyes, but this time the shadowy figure had hands. He started to cry because he didn't know where these images were coming from or what they meant. Just then, the toad popped out of the water, the bird came out of the tree, and the beautiful woman and the woodcutter came out of the forest and sat next to the boy by the pool of water.

They praised the boy for his marvelous gifts and asked him why he was crying.

The boy said, "I see in the water parts of a familiar face and I do not know who it could be."

"Well," asked the toad, "is it me?"

"No," said the boy.

"Is it me?" asked the bird.

"No, it is not you," said the boy.

"Is it me?" asked the beautiful woman.

"No, it is not you either," said the boy.

"Well then," said the woodcutter, "is it me?"

"No, I am sure it is not you either," said the boy.

"Well," the woodcutter said, "let's not worry about this shadowy figure just yet. I think I know who it might be, but you're not ready to know yet. Besides, what we have to tell you is more important. We all have some bad news we must tell."

"Tell me." insisted the boy.

"Well," continued the woodcutter. "In a short while we will all have to leave you, and we will never come back again."

When the boy heard this his heart sank and he said, "But I don't want you to go. I have no other friends, and my uncle laughs and beats me when I use the gifts at home. What am I to do without you?"

"You will know what to do," said the woodcutter. "But we must leave."

"Well," said the boy, "then before you go, let me at least draw you. This way I will remember you."

The beautiful woman then said, "Why don't you also write our stories of how we met in the forest? That way you can tell the stories to others someday."

So the boy set out to write and draw the stories of each of his friends that he met in the forest, starting with the toad. After he drew and wrote about each of the characters, they disappeared. He was now drawing the woodcutter and was just about finished when he stopped.

"I know as soon as I draw you I will be finished and you will disappear. I don't want you to go. You see, you are the first man ever to be my friend."

"Yes, I know that," said the woodcutter. "You see, you are correct, I must leave after you draw me and write my story, but you, my friend, will not be finished until you draw yourself and write your own story."

"But how can I draw myself," asked the boy, "when I don't even know what I look like?"

The woodcutter replied, "When you finish with me, go over to the pool of water and you will see the man you have longed to see and be friends with for so long but were frightened of because you didn't recognize him. You will see your reflection! When you have drawn yourself and have written your story you will be complete, but first, you must finish me."

The boy did what he was told and the woodcutter disappeared after he was drawn. The boy then went over and looked into the pool of water, but he couldn't believe his eyes. He saw a handsome young man who looked very much like the woodcutter who taught him how to hold the sword. As he drew the image he said, "How come it has taken me so long to see you—my reflection in the water?"

To his surprise, the reflection spoke back and said, "It takes time for a man to see himself as he really is. Take your gifts of dance, music, drawing, writing, and sword and go home—someone waits for you there."

The boy ran home and when he entered the cottage he saw his mean cruel uncle dead on the floor. Outside the cottage stood the woodcutter from the forest, only now he was dressed like a king.

"Come," the kingly woodcutter said to the boy. "Let us go from here, my son."

Confused by this, the boy questioned, "But, you are the woodcutter from the forest, how come you are dressed like a king, and why do you call me son?"

"This pin you wear, you received it from your mother, didn't you?" asked the man.

"Yes," replied the boy.

Woodcutter-King then embraced the boy and said, "This pin belongs to the royal family. You see, some eighteen years ago, I fell in love with your mother by the pool of water that gave you your reflection. You, my son, are the result of our love. I promised your mother I would return to her at the pool of water where you learned to dance, play your music, draw, and tell stories. When I saw the pin on your shirt the first day I laid eyes on you, I knew then you were my son, but I also knew, as your father, I had to teach you the ways of being a man. You learned well, my son. Now, you know who you are and all the gifts that you possess. Let us go. Let us leave this house and ride back to our kingdom together as father and son. Your gifts will serve our people well. And one day, you will make a fine king to my throne."

The father and son went back to their kingdom. The boy went on to win many victories for the throne. He killed many dragons with his sword, he wrote many stories about his adventures, he drew pictures of the places he traveled to, and he played music to the delight of the whole kingdom.

It was not long after the death of the king that the boy took the throne. The people would ask him, over and over again, how one man could be blessed with so many gifts. The new king would then take out his storybook and his pictures and he would tell his people the story about the boy who didn't have a reflection.

Three Men and a Road

Once Upon a Time, there were three men all traveling on very different roads that led to the center of life. When they arrived at the center of life and they encountered each other for the first time, they all agreed to sit and rest on the side of the road before they started on the journey once again.

While they sat on the side of the road of life, they asked each other where they had been and where they were heading. Each person shared their stories, and it became obvious that the lessons of life each had experienced, although different, were proving to be beneficial to the other's hearing.

One person spoke of his experience of pain and confusion on the road of life, the other spoke of his experience of thoughtful reflection and understanding on the road of life, and one spoke of his experience of joy and happiness on the road of life. When they were finished sharing their experiences on the road, they each began to argue that their individual road was better than other roads.

Just then, three little boys approached them from the opposite directions and one of them asked, "Why are you arguing about your roads of life?" A second boy added, "Why should any one road be better than the other?" The three men looked at each other with bewilderment. The third boy then said, "We are now all listening. Go ahead and explain your reasons why you think your road is the best."

Being pressed to justify their claim, the three men each took a turn to explain their perceptions.

The first man said, "My road is the best because my life of pain has given me the gift of strength to live."

The second man said, "My road is best because my life of thoughtful reflection and understanding has given me the gift of meaning to live."

The third man said, "My road is best because my life of joy and happiness has given me the gift of hope to live."

As each man heard the other's reasons why their road was the best they were attracted to the other person's road and less satisfied with their own. So each man stood up and looked down the road from which the other had come. To their surprise, instead of seeing three different roads, now there was only one road going back in the direction they had come.

One of the men said, "How can it be possible that there is only one road when each of us experienced three very different roads of life?"

"Do you suppose," the second man said, "that the roads we walked were really one and the same all along?"

The third man looked at the boys who, in response to the men's questions, were now crying, thinking, and laughing, and he asked, "What are you crying, thinking, and laughing about?"

The boys said, "It's not the road but your perception of it that has changed as you heard the stories the others had to tell."

"I don't understand," said the first man, who at this point was in real pain and confused by their words.

The boy who was crying stopped and said, "I'm not surprised you don't understand. You have been lost in your pain and in your pursuit to be made strong for so long that you failed to recognize the joy and the meaning your life could have had as you walked on your road."

Then, the second man interrupted and said, "I think I'm beginning to understand. I guess I should reflect on it a little more."

"That's just your problem," said the boy who was thinking, "you have been so lost in your thoughtful reflection and in your pursuit to find meaning for so long that you failed to recognize the joy and pain of each moment your life could have possessed as you walked on your road."

The third man looked at the boy who was laughing and he started to smile and say, "Yes, life is too short to be so absorbed with pain and serious thought isn't it?"

Suddenly, the third boy stopped laughing and said, "And, that's your problem—you have been so lost in your naive happiness and in your pursuit for joy that you have failed to recognize the strength and insight that comes with thought and pain your life could have brought you as you walked on your road."

The three men were so stunned by the harsh words of these little boys that they were left speechless and they begged the boys to explain what they should now do before they started on their journeys once again.

"Don't you see," said one of the boys, "even though each of you thought you were on different roads you were really next to each other the whole time—it wasn't the road that separated you it was your perception of life."

The second boy said, "It was only possible here, at the center of life's road, where the three of you had a chance to rest from your own journey, that you were able to see and hear your invisible companions because you chose to have your perceptions challenged. And now, it's up to you, when you leave this resting place, how you will let each other teach you about the road of life that waits ahead of you."

The third boy just remained silent as he was waiting for the three men to respond.

The three men looked at each other and then looked at the road ahead. The one road they thought they were on again transformed into three different paths. Needless to say the three men had a look of bewilderment once again. "What is going on here?" the three men cried out.

The third boy spoke, "This is just another trick of your persistent perceptions. There is only one road. Don't you see, if you continue alone with your own perceptions to guide you, you will be walking on separate paths, but if you walk together and share your perceptions and insights into life then no matter what path you walk it will truly be one. Now, we must move on, your road to life is now up to you to live. The choice is yours—either together or alone."

After saying this, the three boys joined arms and walked back in the direction from which the men had come, disappearing as mysteriously as they had arrived.

The three men then searched their hearts and they knew what they had to do if they were going to continue on life's road. They agreed, at least for a while, to walk together on one road. In time, they knew they would learn from each other that the road of life would sometimes be confusing, sometimes enlightening, and sometimes joyful. With the help of the three little boys, the three men grew to believe if they listened to each other and learned from each other all of life's experiences would give them the gifts of strength through pain, meaning through thoughtful reflection, and hope through the love they would share as friends.

Getting up from the side of the road of life, the three men then joined arms, walked slowly on the road ahead, so as not to miss anything they may encounter, and faded gently into the future together.

Let Me Take You Home

I see you standing
by yourself in the dark
I see you crying
afraid to face your heart
I see you've lost your way
as you wander all alone
Don't you see the road you're on
has led you far from home

I see the pain your eyes
try so hard to conceal
I see your broken heart
has forgotten how to feel
I see the mistake you've made
in thinking you're alone
So if you take my hand
I can take you home
Will you let me take you home
Will you say that it's okay
Will you let my love convince you

That I am here to stay
Will you let me hold you close to me tonight
There's no reason you should be alone
Will you let me take you home

I see you running
from the love I want to give
I see you hiding
afraid to let me in
I see the reasons that make you
push my love away
But deep down in your heart
you must trust that I will stay

Will you let me take you home
Will you say that it's okay
Will you let my love convince you
That I am here to stay
Will you let me hold you close to me tonight
There's no reason you should be alone
Will you let me take you home

Bridge

I can take you anywhere
that you want to be
Home is not a place you see
Home is here with me.

The Unfinished House

Once upon a time, there was a house that was in various stages of repair. There were some rooms that had no floor, some rooms had no walls, some rooms were filled with dust, some had tools and supplies, and other rooms were just dark and filled with unmarked boxes from a forgotten past.

Yes, the house was in an unfinished state.

Due to its condition, the house was vulnerable to dampness and cold. The interior of the house was subjected to darkness and somber tones of light. The floor in the house was not sturdy. The walls were just dry wall or unfinished wood. The kitchen still lacked the basic necessities to sustain or provide sufficient nourishment. There was no living space or dining room. The house only provided a bedroom with an old bed and a closet.

What this house needed was a person who would look beyond its surface and see the beautiful dwelling it could become.

One day, a boy entered the unfinished house. The darkness, although frightening at first, soon became mysterious and magical for it was in the darkness of rooms that the boy would imagine a home only his dreams could create.

Letting his dreams take him over, he imagined a beautiful house and then drew what he saw. He would even design in detail each and every room of the house. He hid his dreams and designs in a crack of the floor to keep them safe and then, being tired, he leaned against a wall in a secluded dark room of the house and fell fast asleep. The sleep soon became like the darkness, mysteriously powerful and lasted many years. When the boy finally awoke out of his deep repose he found himself to be a young man. As he looked about the room he wondered where he was and how he got there.

The young man didn't know where he belonged, he felt he had not lived his life and this made him very unhappy. So he took one last walk around the house to see if he could remember, then in his haste to leave the unfinished house, he left behind his dreams and designs buried in a forgotten crack.

He walked outside and looked at the house.

Just then a man walked by and asked, "Is this your house, sir?"

Embarrassed by its appearance, the young man said, "NO!"

The passing man replied, "Oh, that's too bad. You could probably sell this house for some money."

Before the man could continue on his way, the young man asked, "May I ask you a question?"

"Certainly!" was the man's response.

"What should I do to find a place where I belong, where I can really live my life, and where I'll be happy?" the young man asked.

The man responded, "Work and make some money then you will have anything you want."

Being a very talented man it didn't take him long to find work. As time passed, he moved up in career and status. In his pursuit to make money, he worked long hours and didn't think much about anything else. The more he worked the less energy he had and even with all his money he felt he still hadn't found a place to belong, that he still wasn't really living life and he wasn't very happy. Something was missing.

After thinking about his problem for a while, the young man thought, "'I'll go back to where all this started and start again, maybe I've done something wrong." So the man made his way back to the unfinished house.

Just as he got to the door a woman passed by and asked him, "Is this your house, sir?"

Embarrassed by its appearance, the young man said, "NO!"

"Oh, that's too bad." said the woman, "This would be a perfect house for a couple to fix up and spend the rest of their life together in."

And before the woman passed by, the young man asked, "May I ask you something?"

"Certainly." the woman replied.

The young man explained his story and said, "I still don't know where to go to feel like I belong, to feel like I'm living my life and to feel happy."

The woman listened politely and said, "Your problem, sir, is you have to fall in love, if you fall in love, everything you want will come to you."

Being a very pleasant young man it didn't take him long to find someone to fall in love with. Time passed and when the feelings of love wore off, he would move on and find someone else to fall in love with. Now this happened many times. The more he fell in love, the less he trusted it because he knew the feeling wouldn't last and it soon became obvious that he still didn't feel like he belonged anywhere, that he hadn't really lived his life and he knew he wasn't happy. Something was still missing.

So, he decided to go back to where it all started and he made his way back to the unfinished house.

As he approached the unfinished house, an old man passed by and asked, "Is this your house?"

"NO!" said the young man, embarrassed by its appearance.

"Oh, that's too bad." the old man continued. "It's a fine house—it just needs someone to see its beauty and to care for it."

Now, this comment touched the young man in an odd way. The old man could see something in the young man's eyes and he asked, "Is there something wrong?"

"Yes," said the young man. "I have the feeling I'm doing something wrong with my life. I've been trying for some time to feel like I belong, to live my life and to be happy, but nothing works. I've tried work and love but they always leave me feeling unfinished like something's missing. So, I thought I should start again. That's why I'm here at this unfinished house, you see it all started once I stepped outside this door. Can you tell me what to do to find these things I'm looking for?"

"No!" replied the old man. "But you say it all started once you stepped outside the house?"

"Yes." was the young man's reply

"Well, what happened before? What happened inside the house?" the old man asked.

The young man explained, "I don't remember. My memories are all dark and buried. What should I do? I want so badly to belong, to live my life, and to be happy. I just want to start again."

"Well," said the old man, "then you must go back inside the unfinished house. Go back to that dark room and find your memories. Perhaps something you need is still inside the house?"

With that the old man left. The young man once again approached the door and before anyone else passed by he sneaked into the house. The house was just as he left it, cold, damp, dark, unfinished, and yet mysterious too.

He stood in the hallway for quite awhile because he was afraid to enter any room until his eyes adjusted to the darkness.

Once he felt more comfortable with the darkness, he proceeded slowly through the hall. The floor was weak and a few times he feared he would fall through. But he made it to the first room. He looked about—it was a living room, but it was filled with unmarked boxes. The next room had an old bed and a closet. He began to notice windows in the house, so he opened the curtains to let in more light. Because the windows were dirty, he thought, "I suppose I should clean the windows first, this way I'll be able to see better and it'll make it easier to find whatever it is I'm looking for".

Taking off his shirt and using it as a washcloth, he proceeded through the house to see if he could find some access to water. He made his way through a room filled with lumber and building tools. From there he proceeded to a room, which appeared to be a large dining room, but this room was vacant—only dust and dirt on the floor—no table or chairs. Passing through the dining room, he found the bathroom. The sink was disconnected, so using the showerhead, he soaked his shirt—the water, to his surprise, was clean and warm, no rust or dirt seemed to have accumulated in the pipes. "The pipes must be new or of very good quality," he mused. The water felt good as he let some of it hit his face and shoulders.

Then taking his shirt, he proceeded to clean, starting in the kitchen. As he cleaned the glass, more light started filling the room. He noticed the fine detail in the woodwork around the window-sill. There were even a few appliances that seemed to be in working condition. From there he went to each room and cleaned the windows, returning to the shower to rinse out and clean his shirt after each window was washed. In every room, he found something he didn't know was there, once it was exposed by the new light—these discoveries were beautiful.

The dining room had a beautiful inlaid wooden floor, the room with all the tools had a wall with on exotic mural, and the room with all the boxes had a marble fireplace that was in perfect working order. So he thought, "Why not light a fire? Bring some warmth to the house and then I'll continue with the window in the bedroom." He stood in front of the fire—the warmth felt good—and he closed his eyes, thinking, "This house is not as bad as I thought."

With that he entered the bedroom—there was only one window there and he wondered what he would find once the light was let in. Once the window was clean and he turned around the room looked pretty ordinary. A few cracks in the floor. He continued his survey of the room and then he saw it. A figure leaning against the wall in the opposite corner of the room. He slowly approached the figure and when he moved away from the window the light fell right upon the figure. The young man stopped dead in his tracks—the figure leaning against the wall in the opposite corner or the room was a little boy fast asleep.

The young man marveled at this peaceful sight and approached the boy quietly. He bent down to see the youth close up and, just as the young man had his eyes at the level of the sleeping child, the boy opened his eyes and said, "Hello. I've been waiting to meet you. What a wonderful house you have."

The man was tongue-tied, he didn't know what to say. As the boy spoke, he got up, took the man's hand in his, and led him around from room to room saying, "Isn't this a great room, isn't this a neat place?" When they got to the living room, the boy said, "See all these unmarked boxes—they're yours and when the appropriate time comes we will be able to use everything they possess." Noticing the fire, the boy said, "Oh, you lit a fire, it feels wonderful and you've let in more light. I'm so glad you've come home."

The young man wasn't too sure what was going on and shaking his head he finally asked, "Who are you?"

"I'm a little boy." answered the child.

"Well, where do you belong?" the man continued.

"I am here, that must mean I belong with you." was the boy's only explanation.

Before the man could say another word or ask another question the boy excitedly said, "Come here, I have to show you something!" There was great fervor in the boy's voice.

The boy led the man back into the bedroom, he got down on his knees and started lifting up a plank from the floor. The boy then reached his hand into the dark hole and carefully pulled out two pieces of paper: one with sketches and another with detailed designs of every room in the house.

"Look at these!" the boy said as he handed the man his dreams and designs. "This is our house."

As the man took hold of the papers and looked at them, a tremendous feeling of wonder came over him. "The sketches are magnificent and the designs are so thorough. Whose are they?" the man asked.

"They're yours," said the boy. "They belong to you. I've been keeping them safe for you in this crack."

"I don't know what to say." said the man.

"Don't say anything." responded the boy. "I'm just so glad you're home. Now we better get started creating our house. Let's check out the tools and lumber."

To the man's surprise everything with which they would need to repair and build the house he found in the room.

"Where should we start?" asked the man.

"The kitchen." said the boy in a very decisive tone. "I'm very hungry for a good meal."

So off to work they went. The boy described the room in excellent detail just as he saw it in his dreams and designs and the man cut and nailed, scraped and painted, he laid the tile, built the cabinets and hooked up the appliances. In no time, the kitchen was finished. The walls were bright, the floor was clean and every appliance and fixture was in perfect working order. The boy, seeing the room was ready, left the kitchen and started bringing some of the unmarked boxes piled in the living room. Every box, although unmarked, possessed only those objects that were appropriate for a nourishing meal to be prepared and served. As they emptied the boxes, every cabinet, shelf, and drawer got neatly arranged to hold all the objects. When they were finished with the kitchen and when everything was in its proper place, they threw away the boxes, made a good meal, and then retired to the bedroom for a good night's sleep.

Just before falling off to sleep, the man said, "There is so much to do. When will we finish this house?"

The boy simply said, "We'll finish when we're done."

"But when will that be?" Pressed the man.

"When every room is livable. Now don't be preoccupied with when we'll be finished—let's just be content with creating each room as we get there. We'll need to be patient." With that the boy leaned against his corner and fell fast asleep. The man leaned his head against the wall also and, in no time, he too was fast asleep.

In the morning, the boy said to the man, "Get up! Today we must create our dining room." After finding all the tools and equipment they needed in the supply room, they set to work. The boy described the room as he saw it in excellent detail and the man brought it to life. He cut and nailed, scraped and painted, built a table and chairs, and then built a matching cabinet. Then, to finish the job, the man hung a beautiful light from the center of the ceiling that lit up the entire room. Once the light was hung, the boy started to bring some of the boxes piled up in the living room to the dining room. When the cabinets were filled and the table was set they threw away the boxes, prepared a meal, which they ate sitting at the new table, then they retired to the bedroom.

Before they fell asleep, the man said, "I think we'll be finished by the end of the week—what do you think?"

The boy looked at the man across the room and said, "You can't put a time schedule on creating livable rooms. I told you once before, we'll be finished when we're done."

Each morning, the boy would wake up first and call the man to rise. They would then set off creating other rooms and they followed the same routine every day. The boy would describe what his dreams and designs possessed, the man would build. They would then unpack all the unmarked boxes brought by the boy into their appropriate room, and when all was complete they would eat and retire. The man learned not to ask any more questions about finishing—he was content with just creating each room as they got to it.

Eventually, the bathroom was transformed into a healthy place for cleansing and refreshment. The tool room was changed into a guest room with a mural that would both welcome and give comfort to any future visitor, the hallway floor was strengthened and cleaned, and the living room blossomed into a spacious area just right for relaxation, play, and conversation. The unmarked boxes, with the exception of one, had been removed and the furniture left was both functional and attractive for the room. The windows were found to have blinds just suitable so the room could always have the appropriate light shining in or out at any time of day or night.

So, in the morning after all this previous work was done, there was only one room left to finish and only one unmarked box left for that room. Upon rising this time, the man awoke first, he jumped out from the corner, he was feeling very good, and he woke up the boy. He proceeded to make breakfast for the boy, and as they sat at the table eating, the man said, "You know we're almost finished—one more room to go."

The boy just sat there silently.

The man continued, "I don't know how I'll ever thank you for what you have given me."

The boy looked up.

The man continued, "You have given detail that described a place for me to belong, you have given me something to live for that generates my abilities to create things that are beautiful, and you have given me a happiness I haven't experienced before. You gave me your dreams."

"No, I didn't." said the boy. "I just helped you see your own dreams and now, see what you've created?"

After the boy said this, he began to cry.

"What's the matter?" asked the man.

"Nothing." replied the boy. "I'm just happy we had this time together. Thank you for coming home."

"Well, we only have one more room to go, I suppose we should get busy creating." The man said this as he got up from the table and walked back to the unfinished bedroom.

The boy followed behind the man in silence.

When the man entered the room, the boy stood outside the door and said, "We have no more tools, we have no more supplies, we have nothing to create anything else with. Everything has been used."

"Well, then how will we create the unfinished bedroom?" asked the man in a concerned voice.

"I have no more sketches or designs left to describe to you. My dreams are no more." the boy added.

"You mean we won't be able to finish the bedroom?" the man asked.

"Yes, we won't be able to finish the bedroom." the boy said, but then he added, "You'll have to finish it by yourself."

"But how can I do that without the proper tools or supplies, or without your descriptions? Do you think what I need is in the unmarked box?" the man asked.

"Open it and find out." the boy replied.

The man ripped open the box but all he found was a pillow.

"That's it. Just a pillow." was the man's response.

"Yes!" said the boy. "That's all you need to create this room."

"But I don't understand." the man pleaded.

"Don't you see?" said the boy. "On this pillow, you, and not me, will dream from now on. On this pillow, your head will rest with all the possibilities you need to design this room. On this pillow, your mind will create a room that only you will be able to live in. Don't be embarrassed by its appearance now, for only a small number of people will ever see it. Be cautious, however, to whom you show this unfinished room. Some will not like it because it is unfinished. Others will try to fix it for you—don't let them, they don't share or know your dreams. When the right person enters this room, you'll know it because they won't see just an unfinished room with a pillow, they won't try to change it, clutter it up with objects or fix it. They'll see a room filled with dreams yet to be created. But a word of warning. Don't let these people stay in this room for too long even if they see your dreams, for an unfinished room is dark and they may get scared—take them to the other rooms and let them see the beauty your dreams have already created. For the dreams of this room are yours and yours alone—only you can create them. Remember this room is not the house—all the rooms, all the walls, all the floors, and all the dreams combined make this —house what it is. A place to live—Your Home.

So as you sleep tonight, be at peace for your dreams will be safe on this pillow. In the morning, I will be gone, the dreams will be yours and this will be your unfinished room to do with whatever you wish."

Epilogue

As I reflect on the "narrative" of my lifelong career as an educational leader, I am convinced of the transformative power of storytelling in leadership. Each of the forty stories in this collection have served as a beacon of wisdom and inspiration, guiding me and those who encountered them through moments of joy, challenge, and growth.

Using these stories to entertain students while imparting moral lessons has been a privilege and a delight. Seeing the spark of curiosity and understanding light up in their eyes has fueled my commitment to using narrative as a tool for education and empowerment.

I have witnessed the ripple effects of these stories as they inspired parents, teachers, and fellow leaders to embrace change, challenge conventions, and strive for excellence. Through the sharing of these tales, conversations have been sparked, perspectives have shifted, and hearts have been opened to new possibilities. Looking back, I humbly realize that my stories played a pivotal role in creating a culture that valued collaboration and a shared vision of Mission.

Through the transformative journey of storytelling in leadership, I've discovered that personal growth and evolution as a leader are deeply intertwined with the stories we share. Each narrative becomes a mirror reflecting our moments of triumph, vulnerability, and self-discovery, shaping us into the leaders we aspire to be.

To embrace storytelling as a leadership tool, consider sharing not only successes but also challenges and vulnerabilities. Authenticity and vulnerability in storytelling foster genuine connections and empathy, creating a supportive environment where colleagues, students, and loved ones feel empowered to overcome obstacles and pursue growth.

As you embark on your storytelling journey, remember that weaving collective stories into your organization's vision can unite stakeholders toward a common goal. By articulating a compelling vision grounded in shared narratives, leaders reinforce the importance of unity and alignment in achieving success. When colleagues see themselves reflected in these stories, they are more likely to rally together toward a shared purpose.

My hope is that as you journey through these stories, you find resonance, guidance, and inspiration to integrate their timeless lessons into your personal and professional life. May these narratives empower you to inspire and lead with compassion, wisdom, and authenticity, fostering a culture of collaboration based on trust and understanding.

Thank you for joining me on this storytelling adventure. As you continue this journey, may the echoes of these tales accompany you and all you encounter on the path of growth, discovery, and transformation.

Printed in the USA
CPSIA information can be obtained
at www.ICGtesting.com
LVHW040820080924
790207LV00010B/925

9 781963 701135